BREE GOES TO SCHOOL

A Fun and Interactive Children's Book, About,

The First Day of School Jitters,

Friendships and Adjusting to Change

Library of Congress Number: 2021909677

ISBN: 978-1-7372003-1-4

Dedication

This book is dedicated to my
granddaughters, Brianna and Jenna.
Their love of reading and the arts has been
a great inspiration to me.

Bree Goes to School

**A Fun and Interactive Children's Book, About,
The First Day of School Jitters, Friendships
and Adjusting to Change**

It was my first day of school. I held tightly to my mother's hand as we made the short walk from the car to the school. Other children and parents were arriving as well.

Just outside the gate was a tall old man with a short gray beard and a very friendly smile. He had a basket of lollipops hanging from a ribbon around his neck, and the most beautiful parrot sat on his right shoulder.

The old man held out a lollipop in each hand, and he had a big smile, like he was happy to see us. He kept saying, "Good morning, boys and girls. Lollipops anyone?" Some parents stopped to let their children choose lollipops.

There were lots of colors and sizes to choose from. I wanted a big red one, but my mother told me candy was not good for my teeth.

Some children stopped to see the colorful bird and to hear the bird talk. I had never heard a bird talk before. It sounded like a person. It said things like, "Have a lollipop," "Smile," and "Be kind to each other."

The parrot's name was Starr, and the old man, Mr. Moon, had her perform for the children.

Mr. Moon told Starr to go to sleep, and she lay on her belly like she was asleep. Then he asked, "Can you snore?" And she snored, just like my daddy when he sleeps.

This made the children and adults roar with laughter. He told her to wake up, and she woke up and stretched her wings. Then he asked her to laugh out loud, and that bird laughed loudly, like a real person.

The children and their parents laughed out loud too. It was so funny to hear a bird laugh like that. Starr was not only funny, but she was also very beautiful.

After we said goodbye to Mr. Moon and Starr, my mom took me inside to my classroom, where my teacher stood at the door to greet us. I sat at a desk next to a girl who was crying after her mother had left.

"Don't cry, darling," I told her. "Your mommy will be back later."

"My name is not darling," she snapped. "It's Amanda."

"Well, my grandma calls me darling, and it always makes me feel happy. My daddy calls me Tubby, my mommy calls me Sweet Pea, my aunt calls me Boo, my uncle calls me Big Girl—"

"How many names do you have?" interrupted Amanda.

"My real name is Brianna."

"So, may I call you Anna?"

"No. That's what my baby sister calls me. She hasn't learned to say my name yet. But you can call me Bree."

"Okay, Bree. You can call me Mandy—that's what everyone calls me."

We both giggled at all the names.

Sniffles came from the boy at the desk next to Mandy's. Mandy turned her attention to him. "Don't cry," she told him. "Your mommy will be back later. What's your name?" "Jayden," he replied.

"My name is Mandy, and this is my friend Bree."
"Could I be your friend too?" Jayden asked her.
"No!" I yelled. "She is my friend." "But he could be our friend too," said Mandy.

"But I was your friend first." "You will be my best friend, and Jayden will be our friend," said Mandy. "Okay," I agreed.

Just then, Jayden's mother popped her head into the room.

"Jay," she said, "you forgot your lunch."

"Your name is Jay?" Mandy and I said together. We all giggled.

"He seems happy. I was worried about him," Jay's mom said to the teacher, who was still standing by the classroom door.

The bell rang signaling the start of the school day. Mandy and Jay still clutched their lollipops. The teacher asked all the children with lollipops to put them away, then we all stood for the Pledge of Allegiance.

The first day of school was fun. I got to put the sun on the weather chart. Mandy placed the number "65" for the outside temperature. Charles was the weatherman, and he gave the weather report.

That day, our teacher took us for a nature walk in the schoolyard. We stopped under the huge oak trees. Each of us picked up three leaves that had fallen to the ground. Our teacher told us about the seasons of the year, why the leaves fall off the trees, and how the squirrels use the acorns for food, even in the winter.

Later that day, our teacher gave each of us a sheet of paper with our names on it and the outline of three leaves. She let each child choose three colors that they liked, and we got to color our leaves. Soon it was time to go home. We got to take our coloring pages with us.

The next day came quickly. We stopped by to say hello to Mr. Moon and his parrot.

The other children and their parents crowded around—not so much for the lollipops but to admire Starr and to hear her talk and laugh like a real human being. Mr. Moon knew some parents and their children by name.

Back in the classroom, everyone was happy to see each other again.

"My mom put my picture on the refrigerator," Jay said.

"My mom took my picture to work to show her friends," said Mandy.

"My mom showed my dad my picture as soon as he walked in the door, and my dad said he was very proud of me," I said.

Not to be outdone, Sarah, the girl who sat behind me, chimed in, "Well, my mom FaceTimed both my grandmas, and they both were very proud of me."

"Oh no," wailed Nicholas.

"What's wrong, Nick?" Mandy asked.

"I forgot to give my dad my picture when he picked me up. It's still in my bag."

"Don't worry," I said. "Just remember to give it to him today."

29

When school started, Sheena was the weatherwoman. Jay was upset because he wanted to do it. He thought only boys should be weathermen and tried to take the pointer from her.

First, our teacher reminded him what Starr, the parrot, said—to be kind to each other. Then, she told the class that we can become anything we want when we grow up. The teacher asked the class what we would like to become when we grow up.

Movie Star
Lawyer
President
Jewele
Nurse
Fireman
Doctor
Pilo

Charles wanted to be a doctor like his dad and make sick people well. Jay wanted to become a pilot and fly huge jets high in the sky. Sheena wanted to become a model and be on television and on the cover of magazines.

I said I wanted to become President of the United States. Mark wanted to be a jeweler and a football player. Some children wanted to become lawyers, teachers, nurses, firemen, and police officers. Matt had not made up his mind what he wanted to become.

Our teacher said some children need more time to decide and that some even change their minds as they grow older.

First, I was scared to go to school, but school is so much fun. We learn a lot, we get to do fun things, we make new friends, and each morning, always there by the gate to greet us and make us laugh is good old Mr. Moon with his beautiful parrot, Starr.

www.ingramcontent.com/pod-product-compliance
Lightning Source LLC
Chambersburg PA
CBHW041542240626
47164CB00002B/94

* 9 7 8 1 7 3 7 2 0 0 3 1 4 *